A Whole Basketball Game . . . Gone!

"Where's the camera?" Joe asked.

The boys searched around the rows of lockers. Suddenly Frank saw something shiny and silver. "There it is!" he called.

The camera was on a bench in a deserted corner of the locker room.

"Boy, are we lucky," Frank told Joe. "If that thing disappeared, you would have been toast."

Joe picked up the camera. He popped open the tape slot.

"I still am toast," Joe said slowly.

Frank and Chet came over to look at the camera. Joe shook it upside down. "The tape of the tryouts is missing!"

Frank and Joe Hardy: The Clues Brothers

Available from MINSTREL BOOKS

JUMP SHOT
DETECTIVES

Franklin W. Dixon

Illustrated by
Marcy Ramsey

A
MINSTREL®
BOOK

Published by POCKET BOOKS
New York   London   Toronto   Sydney   Tokyo   Singapore

This book is a work of fiction. Names, characters, places and incidents are products of the author's imagination or are used fictitiously. Any resemblance to actual events or locales or persons, living or dead, is entirely coincidental.

A MINSTREL PAPERBACK *Original*

A Minstrel Book published by
POCKET BOOKS, a division of Simon & Schuster Inc.
1230 Avenue of the Americas, New York, NY 10020

Copyright © 1998 by Simon & Schuster Inc.

Front cover illustration by Thompson Studio

Produced by Mega Books, Inc.

ISBN: 0-671-00405-0

First Minstrel Books printing January 1998

10 9 8 7 6 5 4 3 2 1

Printed in the U.S.A.

1

Foul Play

What an exciting afternoon, folks," eight-year-old Joe Hardy said into the microphone of his video camera. "The tryouts for the Bayport Elementary School basketball team are about to begin!"

Joe's nine-year-old brother, Frank, walked over and turned off the camera. "Save it for the game, squirt."

"I may be a squirt," Joe said with a grin, "but I'm going to be one awesome sportscaster."

It was Friday afternoon. Frank was going to try out for the basketball team. Joe was going to use the Hardy family's video camera to tape the tryouts for Coach Caruso. The coach had hurt his back and had to stay in bed for a whole week.

Joe looked around the Bayport Elementary School gym. The bleachers were filled with parents and friends of the boys and girls trying out for the team.

"There's Mom!" Frank said, waving.

Mrs. Hardy waved back. Then she gave the boys the thumbs-up sign.

Frank and Joe knew many of the kids trying out for the team, which was called the Bayport Gulls. The assistant coach, Mr. Martinez, had handed out red T-shirts to half the kids trying out. He had given blue T-shirts to the other half. All the kids trying out for the team were going to play in a real game.

"Who's the guy with the attitude?" Joe said, looking at a dark-haired boy in a blue T-shirt. The boy was running and dribbling a basketball really fast.

"That's Peter Libretti. He's in my class," Frank said. "Everyone calls him Dribbles."

Joe watched Dribbles slam-dunk the ball into the basket.

"Fancy," Joe said.

"Don't remind me," Frank said. "He's on the blue team. I'm on the red."

A boy lugging a big knapsack waved from across the gym. It was the Hardys' friend Mike Mendez. Mike was in Joe's class at school.

Mike didn't really like sports. He liked to spend his time inventing things like automatic birdcage cleaners.

"Hi, Mike. Didn't Chet say he'd be here, too?" Frank asked when Mike walked over. Chet Morton was the Hardys' other good friend. Chet was in Frank's class at school.

"Chet's over there," Mike said. He pointed to a large, feathery creature running across the gym and flapping his wings.

"*Arrrrrk! Arrrrrk!*"

"Is that Chet?" Frank laughed. "Way to go!"

"Chet is trying out for Gulliver, the team mascot," Mike explained. "If he does a good job today, he'll get to be mascot all year long."

Chet flapped over to his friends. "Greetings, boys and gulls! *Arrk! Arrk!*"

Joe pointed the video camera at Chet. "What's it like inside that thing?" he asked.

"Great. Except for one thing," Chet said.

"What?" Joe asked, tapping the long orange beak on Chet's mask.

Chet held up a bag of Cheezy Wheezies. "I can't reach my mouth!"

Frank, Mike, and Joe laughed. They knew that Chet loved to eat more than anything.

"Is that camera hard to work?" Chet asked Joe.

"It's a cinch," Joe said. "I just point it at someone, push the button, then ask a million questions."

Joe turned the camera on Frank. "Frank Hardy? How does it feel to be the star of Bayport Elementary School?" he asked.

Frank felt someone give him a shove. It was Dribbles Libretti. He dribbled a ball in circles around Frank.

"There's only one basketball star in this school—*me!*" Dribbles shouted into the camera.

Joe pretended to wipe the camera lens. "Do they call you Dribbles because of the way you shoot hoops, or because of the way you spit when you talk?"

Chet yanked the bulky mask from his head and began to laugh. "Ha! Ha!"

Dribbles glared at Chet. "What's so funny, birdbrain?" Suddenly Dribbles

5

threw back his head and began to sneeze.

"Gesundheit, Libretti," Frank said.

"I'll see you on the court, Hardy," Dribbles said, then sniffled. As Dribbles walked away, Frank and Joe saw the school's initials stenciled on the back of his head with green hair goop.

"Ignore him, Frank," Mike said. "Dribbles Libretti is bad news."

Chet tugged at Mike's knapsack. "What's in this thing anyway, dinosaur bones?"

"Better than that," Mike said. "It's something I invented for Frank."

"What is it?" Frank asked eagerly.

Mike unzipped his knapsack. He pulled out a pair of sneakers. "Ta-daa!"

"Thanks," Frank said, lifting his foot. "But I already have sneakers."

"These aren't just *any* sneakers," Mike said. "These sneakers have springs on the soles. They make you jump higher."

Frank, Joe, and Chet stared at Mike.

"You can use them to score baskets," Mike went on. "I can make pairs for the whole team."

"Weird," Chet said with a laugh. "Sneakers with springs on the soles!"

"Hey, I'm serious," Mike said.

"They're great, Mike," Frank said. "But I don't think Coach will go for them."

"Besides," Joe said, "the name of the team is the Bayport Gulls—not the Bayport Grasshoppers."

"Very funny!" Mike snapped. Then he walked away angrily.

"Wow," Chet said. "He sure took that hard."

Just then Mr. Martinez blew his whistle. "All players on the court!" he called.

"This is it, you guys," Frank said.

"That means me, too!" Chet cried. He pulled on his mask. Then he ran in front of the bleachers and began to dance.

"Go, Gulliver! Go, Gulliver! Go, Gulliver!" the crowd chanted.

7

Mr. Martinez selected five players for each starting team.

Joe turned the camera on. "The players are heading onto the court."

Suddenly a woman with bright orange hair jumped in front of the camera lens.

"Hello, Coach Caruso," she sang with a wave. "Get well soon!"

Joe shut off the camera. He looked up to see Mrs. Saris, who owned Pizza Paradise on Bay Street. Her son, Kevin, was trying out for the team. Kevin was in Joe's third-grade class at school.

"Hi, Mrs. Saris," Joe said. "Let me get a shot of that sweatshirt." Mrs. Saris's sweatshirt had the words Go, Kevin written all over it.

"Keep the camera on Kevin at all times," Mrs. Saris told Joe. "I want the coach to see how well he plays."

Then Mrs. Saris waved and ran back to the bleachers.

I can't do that, Joe thought. Not for all the pepperoni pizzas in the world!

Joe knew almost everyone on the red team. Frank and a boy named Malcolm from Joe's class were guards. Kevin Saris and Tanya Wilkins, a girl from the fourth grade, were forwards. Zack Jackson, the bully of Bayport, was center.

"This is Joe Hardy with the play-by-play," Joe said when the game began. "The blue team has the ball, and they break for the hoop."

Joe followed the action carefully. "Dribbles Libretti is doing what he does best—dribbling the ball to the basket."

A fifth-grade girl on the blue team waved her arms for Dribbles to pass the ball. But Dribbles didn't pass it to anyone.

"Folks, it looks like Dribbles is hot-dogging!" Joe said as he pointed the camera at the court. "What will Mr. Martinez say about that?"

Joe glanced away from the camera. Mr. Martinez was standing behind Chet and shouting. "Step aside! I can't see!" he called.

Gulliver was jumping in front of Mr. Martinez, waving his feathered arms in Mr. Martinez's face.

Joe turned the camera back to the game. Frank was receiving the ball. "Frank Hardy has control of the ball! Dribbles tries to block the shot—"

Just then Joe saw something that made his mouth drop open. Dribbles's foot was in Frank's way.

Sure enough, Frank tripped over the huge sneaker. "Oof," he moaned. Then he fell to the floor with a thud.

2

Trouble on Tape

Frank!" Joe cried, shutting off the camera. He could see his mom stand up in the bleachers.

"Are you okay, sport?" Mr. Martinez asked as Frank stood up.

"I'm okay," Frank said, straightening his T-shirt. "No thanks to Bigfoot here."

"Who are you calling Bigfoot?" Dribbles demanded.

Frank turned to Mr. Martinez. "He tripped me. That's a foul."

12

"I didn't see a thing, I'm afraid," Mr. Martinez said. He glanced at Chet. "A little birdie got in my way."

"Sorry," Chet said with a shrug. "I think I got carried away."

Dribbles folded his arms across his chest. "Frank was just being a klutz."

Frank glared at Dribbles.

"You tripped him," Joe said, marching over to Dribbles. "And I have the whole thing on tape!"

"Let me see that," Dribbles said. He reached for the camera.

"No way," Joe said, pulling the camera away. "But Coach Caruso will see it first thing on Monday."

"He will not!" Dribbles shouted.

"Will so!" Joe shouted back.

Mr. Martinez blew his whistle for quiet. He pointed to Dribbles.

"Libretti, shape up or you're out of the tryouts."

Dribbles scowled and looked at the floor.

"Everyone take their positions," Mr. Martinez announced. "And let's get on with the game!"

Mr. Martinez passed the ball to the red team, and the game continued. Dribbles behaved himself, but he kept making faces at the camera.

I wish I could edit him out, Joe thought.

During the second quarter, the game got really exciting.

"Frank Hardy receives the ball!" Joe cried. "He dribbles toward the basket. He shoots—and it's in! Frank Hardy scores!"

Chet led the crowd in a chorus of "Hardy! Hardy! Hardy!"

During the third quarter, Kevin, Tanya, and a third grader from the blue team were taken out so that other players could try out.

"Is that tape really for Coach Caruso?" Kevin asked Joe.

"You bet," Joe said. "The coach is going to use it to choose the team."

"Is there any way to cut me out of the tape?" Kevin asked.

"Cut you out?" Joe asked.

"Just the part where I'm being thrown out of the game," Kevin pleaded.

Joe shook his head. "Coach Caruso wants to see everything. Besides, you weren't thrown out of the game. Mr. Martinez just wants to give everyone a chance to try out."

"Explain that to my mom," Kevin mumbled, looking up at the bleachers.

Mrs. Saris was standing up and chanting, "We want Kevin! We want Kevin!"

"Sorry, Kevin." Joe sighed.

"That's okay," Kevin said. Then he walked away.

The fourth quarter had everyone on their feet. Dribbles scored two points and brought the blue team to victory.

"The blue team wins the game," Joe announced into the camera. "But who

16

will wear the Gulls uniform? Only Coach Caruso will know for sure. This is Joe Hardy, signing off."

Frank ran over to the bench, out of breath.

"Great game," Joe said to Frank.

"It was," Frank said, "except for the part where Dribbles tripped me."

Frank looked around the gym for Dribbles, but he was nowhere in sight.

"You probably made the team, anyway," Joe said. He patted his camera. "Besides, the truth about Dribbles will come out when we look at the tape."

Frank and Joe saw Mrs. Hardy across the gym. She was chatting with Tanya's parents.

"I'm thirsty," Frank said. "Let's get something from the snack table."

Joe saw Chet standing at the door leading to the locker room. He was still wearing the Gulliver costume.

"Hey, Chet!" Joe called. "Want something to eat?"

Chet shook his large bird-head no.

"That's weird," Frank said. "Chet Morton—not hungry?"

Joe shrugged. He walked over to Chet and handed him the camera. "Hold the camera while we go get some snacks."

Joe thought he heard Chet mumble, "Sure," through his mask.

Frank and Joe walked to the snack table. There were bottles of juice and plates of cookies and pretzels.

"The oatmeal cookies look good," Frank said to Joe.

Just then another kid looked up from the table. He wore a sweatshirt and jeans, and he was reaching for some cookies. "Try the chocolate chip. They're awesome."

"Chet?" Joe gasped. "How could you be here when you were just over there— in your Gulliver costume?"

"What are you talking about?" Chet asked.

"How long have you been standing here?" Frank asked.

Chet popped a cookie in his mouth. "Since the game ended. I was the first one at the snack table," he said proudly.

"What happened to your Gulliver costume?" Joe asked.

Chet shrugged. "I left it in the locker room. That thing was so hot. Besides, I was starved."

"The camera!" Frank and Joe shouted together.

The brothers turned and ran to the locker room.

"What's going on?" Chet called as he followed Frank and Joe.

"Someone was wearing the Gulliver costume," Frank called over his shoulder.

"And that person has our camera," Joe added.

The boys charged into the locker room. They looked around. It was empty.

"There's Gulliver," Chet said. The bird costume and mask lay on the floor.

"But where's the camera?" Joe asked, his voice shaking.

The boys searched around the rows of lockers. Suddenly Frank saw something shiny and silver. "There it is!" he called.

The camera was on a bench in a deserted corner of the locker room.

"Boy, are we lucky," Frank told Joe. "If that thing disappeared, you would have been toast."

Joe picked up the camera. He popped open the tape slot.

"I still am toast," Joe said slowly.

Frank and Chet walked over to Joe. They looked down at the camera.

Joe shook the camera upside down. "The tape of the tryouts is missing!"

3

Mystery Mascot Mess

"If Coach Caruso doesn't see the tryouts, he'll never be able to pick a team," Frank said.

"Or a mascot," Chet moaned.

Frank paced back and forth. "I'll bet the person who took the tape was the same person inside the mascot costume."

"Yeah, the person who I gave the camera to," Joe added. "I wonder who it was."

"Probably Dribbles," Frank said. "He

didn't want you to show that tape to the coach on Monday."

Joe nodded. "And he disappeared right after the game."

"Who else could have wanted the tape?" Chet asked.

Joe snapped his fingers. "Kevin Saris didn't want Coach Caruso to see the tape either."

"It can't be Kevin," Chet said. "I saw him at the snack table after the game. He was eating a frosted doughnut."

Joe sat down on a bench. He rested his head in his hands. "What do we do now?"

"Hmm," Frank said. "I guess we'll have to investigate."

Chet rubbed his hands. "Another case for the Clues Brothers. Yes!"

"I wish Dad weren't away on a case this week," Joe said. "We could use his help."

The boys' dad, Fenton Hardy, was a

private detective in Bayport. He usually helped Frank and Joe with their cases.

"Dad will be back on Sunday night," Frank said.

"We'd better find the tape by then," Joe said. "Coach Caruso needs it first thing Monday morning."

Just then some boys came into the locker room to get their coats.

"Let's search the place before it fills up," Frank whispered. "Maybe the thief left some clues."

The boys looked around the locker room. Joe saw that the exit door was open.

"Whoever was wearing the costume probably ran out that door when they heard us coming," Joe said.

"If they left in a hurry, maybe they left behind a clue for us," Frank said. He took the Gulliver costume from Chet. He looked at the sleeves, the legs, and the gloves.

"Bingo!" Frank cried. He pulled a red plastic ring from one of the gloves.

"That's a decoder ring. I don't have a ring like that," Chet said. "Where'd it come from?"

"It probably belonged to the mystery person inside the Gulliver costume," Joe said, staring at the ring.

Frank slipped the ring into his pocket. "Okay, now we have clue number one."

"Let's go back out to the gym," Chet said. "I want some more cookies. Are there any more clues around here?"

Joe pointed to the floor under his feet. "You're standing in one."

Chet looked down. His sneaker was surrounded by a bright green puddle.

"Gross!" Chet cried. "What is it?"

Joe bent down to examine the puddle. "It looks like the same green hair goop that Dribbles had in his hair."

"This is good evidence," Frank told Chet. "Don't clean your sneakers."

Chet shrugged. "No problem."

24

"So," Frank said, "we have the decoder ring and the green goop. What else can we take home as evidence?"

"I wish we could check out the Gulliver costume more," Joe said. "But it's too big to get out of here."

Chet tossed Frank the Gulliver glove. "Why don't you just take the glove? Nobody's going to miss it over the weekend."

"Thanks," Frank told Chet. "Meet us in the park tomorrow morning at ten. We'll map out our plans there."

"We'd better go find Mom," Joe said. "She's probably looking for us."

The boys got their coats from their lockers. They took their combination locks and headed out of the door.

"You're very lucky the camera wasn't stolen," Mrs. Hardy said after Joe told her what happened.

"Tell me about it," Joe said. "But the tape is important, too, Mom."

"It certainly is," Mrs. Hardy said. "I'm

afraid it's your responsibility to find it."
Then she smiled at Frank and Joe. "And
I know you will."

The next day was Saturday, but Frank
and Joe were up bright and early. They
got dressed quickly. Then they went
downstairs to the den, which their father
used as his office.

"Dad has so many detective books,"
Joe said. He twisted the brim of his base-
ball cap to the back. "I'm sure one of the
books will help us."

Frank reached for a book on the second shelf. "Here's the one I was looking for."

"This book belonged to Dad when he
was our age," Frank said. "It's called, *So
You Want to Be a Detective?* It tells all
about how real detectives solve crimes."

Joe took the book from Frank and
opened it. "Wow. It even has chapters
on fingerprints and scent hounds!"

"If we do everything by the book, we can't lose," Frank said.

Frank slipped the book in his pocket. Then the brothers headed to the kitchen for breakfast.

"I'm going to call Mike," Joe said as they passed the telephone in the hall. "Just to make sure he's not mad at us for laughing at his sneaker invention."

Joe picked up the phone and dialed Mike's number. The phone rang three times before Mike picked it up.

"Hello?"

"Hey, Mike," Joe said cheerily. "It's me, Joe—"

Click!

Joe stared at the receiver. "Mike?"

"What happened?" Frank asked.

"Mike just hung up on me," Joe said. "I guess he's still mad at us."

Frank thought for a moment. "Do you think he was mad enough to steal the tape?"

"Mike Mendez?" Joe said. "No way. Why would he do that?"

Frank shrugged. "To get back at us for laughing at him."

Joe shook his head. "Mike wouldn't do something like that—would he?"

The boys walked into the kitchen. A box of cereal called Crispy Creatures was sitting on the table.

"Yuck!" Joe said after tasting a spoonful. "This stuff tastes like dirty socks!"

Frank looked at the front of the box. "Isn't Crispy Creatures Mike's favorite brand?"

Joe nodded. "I don't know how he eats three boxes of this stuff a week."

"It must offer a great prize," Frank said. He looked at the back of the box. " 'Crispy Creatures Decoder Ring for Just Ten Box Tops,' " he read out loud.

Frank stared at the picture of the ring. "Hey. This is the same ring we found inside the Gulliver glove!"

Joe stretched his neck to look at the box. He could tell it was the same ring.

"Anyone who eats so much Crispy Creatures," Joe said slowly, "must have a Crispy Creatures decoder ring."

"You *do* know what that means, don't you?" Frank asked.

Joe nodded. "It means that Mike Mendez might be the thief after all!"

4

Cheezy Wheezies to Sneezies!

We've got to find Chet and tell him about the Crispy Creatures ring," Frank told Joe after Mrs. Hardy dropped them off at the park.

"Speaking of creatures," Joe said, pointing to the basketball court. "Look who's shooting hoops."

Dribbles Libretti was jumping in front of a younger boy and blocking his shot. Dribbles's own basketball lay on the side of the court.

"Why don't you play with your own basketball?" the boy demanded. "This one's mine."

Dribbles grabbed the boy's basketball and shot it over the boy's head. "Not anymore!"

Frank shook his head. "I know he took the tape," he whispered to Joe. "I just know it."

"But how can we prove it?" Joe asked.

Just then a small black dog ran through Frank's legs. The dog was chasing a gray squirrel.

"A dog—that's it!" Joe cried. "Give me the detective book."

Frank pulled the book from his pocket and tossed it to Joe.

"Scent dogs," Joe said. "They could sniff the mascot glove and lead us straight to the person who was wearing the costume."

"Where are we going to find a dog that can sniff out clues?" Frank asked.

Joe thought for a second. "Tony Prito

told me he has a dog. And he brings him here to the park every Saturday morning."

Tony was the Hardys' new friend. He was in Joe's third-grade class.

Frank and Joe found Tony on the other side of the park. He was watching a group of skateboarders.

"Boof would be perfect," Tony said, after Joe explained everything. "He's fast as a rocket and as strong as a superhero."

"The important question is," Frank said, "how does he smell?"

Tony shrugged. "Sometimes pretty bad."

"No," Frank said. "I mean, how is his nose? Can he sniff out clues?"

"Why don't you take him on a test run?" Tony asked. Then he cupped his hands around his mouth and yelled, "Boof! Come out, come out, wherever you are."

A huge gray-and-white sheepdog

poked his head around a tree. His fluffy ears perked up when he saw the Hardys.

"Wow," Frank said. "I think he'll do."

"Woof!" Boof barked.

In no time, Frank, Joe, and Tony were being dragged through the park by a joyful Boof.

"We're supposed to be walking *you!*" Frank told Boof as he tugged the leash.

"I told you he was strong," Tony said.

After walking a few more feet, Frank pulled the Gulliver glove from his jacket pocket.

"This is where the glove comes in handy," Frank said with a smile. He held it under Boof's nose. "Here, boy. Take a good whiff."

Boof nuzzled the glove with his nose. Then he took off like a flash of lightning.

"There he goes!" Tony shouted.

"He's heading for the basketball court," Frank shouted.

"I knew it," Joe cried, waving his arms. "He's tracked down Dribbles."

"Way to go, Boof," Tony shouted.

The boys chased Boof onto the basketball court.

"Get a load of the dust mop!" Dribbles laughed, waving the basketball in front of Boof. But instead of chasing Dribbles, Boof ran right past him.

"Where's he going?" Joe said.

Boof led the boys to the playground. The dog ran around the swings and skidded to a stop by the jungle gym.

"Woof! Woof! Woof! Woof!" Boof barked.

"Boof tracked someone down," Joe said.

"Oh, no," Frank said, staring up at the jungle gym. "It's Chet!"

5

That's a Print

Chet was sitting near the top bar of the jungle gym. His seven-year-old sister, Iola, was sitting two bars down.

"What a big, friendly doggy!" Iola squealed.

Frank noticed that Chet was clutching a bag of Cheezy Wheezies.

"Ah-ha!" Frank cried. "When Boof sniffed the glove, he probably smelled the Cheezy Wheezies crumbs from yesterday."

"That's why he ran straight for Chet," Joe agreed.

"Calm down, you big mutt!" Chet called to Boof.

"He's not a mutt," Tony said angrily. "He's an English sheepdog."

"Then why doesn't he understand English?" Chet wailed.

"Chet!" Frank called up. "Throw Boof your bag of Cheezy Wheezies."

"No way!" Chet shouted. "They're nacho-flavored—my favorite."

Iola scrambled up and grabbed the bag from Chet. Then she tossed it down to Boof. He nuzzled the bag playfully.

Suddenly Dribbles Libretti pushed his way between Frank and Joe.

"Hey, Morton," Dribbles said, twirling his basketball on his index finger. "That dog eats more junk than you. Ha, ha!"

The boys and Iola glared at Dribbles as he strutted away.

"Twerp," Chet mumbled.

Iola jumped down from the jungle

gym. She faced Frank and Joe. "Chet told me all about the missing tape. Can I help you find it?"

"I guess so," Frank said. "We can use all the help we can get."

"And Boof here could use a bath," Tony said, tugging at Boof's collar. "His fur is full of Cheezy Wheezies."

Chet shook his head. "He didn't even eat them. What a waste."

"So long, you guys," Tony said with a wave. "And thanks for making my dog a secret agent." Then Tony walked Boof out of the playground.

Frank took out the detective book. "Okay. Let's see what we can try next."

Joe looked over Frank's shoulder as Frank flipped through the pages of the book.

"Fingerprints," Frank said finally. "If we can get a copy of Dribbles's fingerprints, we can compare them to the ones on the video camera."

"And if they match," Joe said, "it

proves that Dribbles had the camera. And maybe even took the tape."

Frank leaned against the jungle gym. "How are we going to get Dribbles's fingerprints?"

Chet shrugged. "We can wait until he punches someone in the nose."

Iola's eyes opened wide. "When I was in line at the water fountain, I heard Dribbles tell someone that he had to go to the library today. We could get his fingerprints off a library book."

"It's worth a shot," Frank said.

Frank, Joe, Chet, and Iola left the park. When they reached the Bayport Library, they entered the Children's Reading Room.

"Anybody see Dribbles?" Joe asked as he looked around.

Mr. Kowalski, the librarian, looked up from his desk. He tapped his lips with his finger. "Shh!"

They tiptoed around the library, searching for Dribbles.

"There he is," Chet whispered.

Dribbles was standing at the copy machine. He was copying pages from a book. His basketball rested against his big foot.

"Look," Chet said. "He still has the green stuff on the back of his head."

"Eeewwww—gross!" Iola said.

Dribbles finished what he was doing. He scooped up his book, papers, and the basketball. Then he walked away to the tables.

"Let's check out the copier," Frank suggested. "Maybe he left something on the glass."

Frank, Joe, Chet, and Iola scurried over to the machine. Frank carefully lifted the cover.

"He sure did leave something." Frank pointed to the glass. "Lots of smudges from his dirty hands."

"And his fingerprints," Joe added with excitement.

"Are we lucky or what?" Iola asked.

"Watch this," Chet said. He popped a quarter into the copier and pressed the green button. A copy of Dribbles's hands slid out on the tray.

Joe grabbed the paper and looked at it. "The fingerprints came out perfectly," he said.

"Awesome," Frank said.

Just then Dribbles appeared behind them. He held his basketball under his arm.

"What's that?" Dribbles asked, pointing to the paper in Joe's hand.

Iola stepped up to Dribbles. "If you must know, they're fingerprints."

Frank groaned. "Iola!"

Dribbles stared at the paper. "Oh, yeah?"

A wicked smile came over his face. Then he turned to the librarian and shouted out: "Mr. Kowalski! Mr. Kowalski! Come here right away. These kids are making copies of their hands!"

6

Slam Dunk Suspect

Oh, great!" Joe groaned. He stuffed the copy of Dribbles's fingerprints in his jacket pocket.

"See ya!" Dribbles waved back as he walked out of the library.

"Is that true? Are you kids making copies of your hands?" Mr. Kowalski asked when he came over.

"No, we weren't," Frank insisted.

"We were making copies of—somebody else's hands," Chet blurted out.

Frank nudged Chet with his elbow.

"This machine is for copying papers,"
Mr. Kowalski said. "Not hands, feet, or
noses."

"We're sorry, Mr. Kowalski," Frank
said. "It won't happen again."

Frank, Joe, Chet, and Iola hurried out
of the library. Just outside the front door,
they saw Dribbles bouncing his basketball on the stone steps.

"Why did you want my fingerprints?"
Dribbles asked with a sneer. "So you can
see what a real champ's hands look
like?"

Frank marched over to Dribbles. "It
was *you* who stole the tape of the tryouts
yesterday, wasn't it?"

Dribbles stopped bouncing. "Tape?
What tape?"

"The tape for Coach Caruso," Joe explained. "It's missing."

"Missing?" Dribbles cried. Then he
laughed. "That means the coach won't

see Frank fall flat on his face. What a shame!"

Frank pulled out the Gulliver glove. He held it under Dribbles's nose. "Look familiar?"

Chet paced back and forth. "And where were you yesterday afternoon after the tryouts?"

Dribbles stared at the glove. Suddenly a frightened look came over his face.

"Get that thing away from me!" he shouted. He began to sneeze. "Ah-chooo! Ah-chooo! I'm allergic to f-f-feathers!"

Frank stared at the glove. "Allergic to feathers?"

"Yeah!" Dribbles sniffled. He put the basketball in front of his face. "I can't even wear a down jacket." He sneezed again.

Frank turned to Joe. "Come to think of it, Dribbles *did* sneeze yesterday when Chet was in the Gulliver costume."

Dribbles grabbed his basketball and

ran down the steps. Halfway down, he bumped into Kevin Saris.

"Outta my way!" Dribbles shouted as he ran off.

"Hi, Kevin!" Frank called. "Want to shoot some hoops later?"

Kevin shook his head fast. "Maybe some other time," he said as he ran inside the library.

"He sure is acting strange," Joe said.

"Yeah," Frank said. "Maybe we should put him on our suspect list."

Chet waved his arms. "I told you guys, Kevin was at the snack table. He was eating a frosted doughnut—with chocolate sprinkles."

Joe nodded. "Oh, right."

"And speaking of food, I could use some lunch," Chet said.

Chet and Iola left to go home for lunch. Frank and Joe returned to their house, too.

"Dribbles is allergic to feathers," Joe said as he plopped down on the bed in

Frank's room. "So, he probably wouldn't go near the Gulliver costume."

Frank reached for a large box on his game shelf. "I won't count Dribbles out until we dust the camera for his fingerprints."

Joe looked at the box and smiled. "The Do-It-Yourself Detective Kit. Cool!"

Mr. Hardy had given Frank the junior detective kit for his ninth birthday.

Frank took a jar of black powder and a small feather duster from the box. "I'll bet these are the tools that real detectives use to dust for fingerprints."

Frank and Joe read the instructions. Then Joe placed the video camera on a piece of newspaper.

"All systems go," Frank said. He sprinkled some black powder on the side of the camera. After a few seconds, he brushed away the excess powder with a feather duster.

"Presto!" Frank said. "The fingerprints appear."

"But are they *Dribbles's* fingerprints?" Joe asked.

"Let's see," Frank said. He compared the fingerprints on the camera to the ones from the copy machine.

"No match." Frank sighed.

"Now what do we do?" Joe wondered out loud. "Dribbles was our number one suspect."

"He still is," Frank said. "There's one more thing we have to do."

"What?" Joe asked.

"The detective book has a whole chapter on testing evidence," Frank explained.

"You mean like the green goop on the locker-room floor?" Joe asked.

Frank smiled. "Exactly!"

After lunch Frank and Joe got permission to ride their bikes to the Mortons' house. Chet and Iola were waiting with a bottle of bright green hair color.

"Are you sure this is the same hair goop that Dribbles uses?" Chet asked in the upstairs bathroom. He had a yellow towel draped around his neck.

Frank looked at the label on the bottle. "It says this is 'hair-raising color.' I once heard Dribbles tell someone that he wears this brand."

"Then let's do it," Iola said. She took the bottle from Frank. She slowly squeezed the goop over Chet's head.

"Yuck!" Chet wailed as Iola slopped the bright green color through his hair.

"Don't worry. I know what I'm doing," Iola said. "I bought this stuff last Halloween for my vampire costume."

Frank smiled. "Now we'll get to compare the hair dye to the gunk we found on the locker-room floor."

"Why do we have to put it in *my* hair?" Chet complained.

Joe shrugged. "This is what detectives-in-training do."

"Done!" Iola cried as she snapped off her rubber gloves. She held a small mirror in front of Chet's face.

Chet's mouth dropped open. "I look like a green lollipop!"

They waited a few minutes for the color to set in. Then Frank held Chet's green-stained sneaker next to his head.

"It doesn't look like the green stuff we found in the locker room," Frank said. "The stuff on your hair is darker."

Joe asked Chet to shake his head back and forth. "And it doesn't drip either," Joe said.

"I guess that rules out Dribbles completely." Frank sighed. "It leaves us with Mike Mendez."

"And it leaves me with gunk in my hair. Can I wash it now?" Chet asked.

Frank and Joe nodded.

"Great!" Chet exclaimed. He turned to Iola. "How does this stuff come out anyway?"

Iola folded her arms across her chest and shrugged. "It doesn't!"

7

Secrets, Lies, and Pizza Pies

What do you mean, it doesn't come out?" Chet shouted.

"Well, it does—eventually," Iola said. "But you have to wash your hair about six times."

Chet took the towel off his shoulders. "I hate to wash my hair!"

Frank turned to Iola. "I thought you bought this hair color for your Halloween costume."

"I did," Iola answered. "But I never

used it," she added with a smile. "Who wants to be stuck with green hair forever?"

"Mom will have a cow when she sees me like this!" Chet wailed.

"Thanks for helping us, big guy," Joe said, slapping Chet on the back.

"What are we going to do next?" Iola asked, her eyes shining.

Frank thought for a moment. "Let's meet in front of Mike Mendez's house tomorrow morning. I want to talk to him about the missing tape."

Chet nodded. "I'll be there."

"Not me," Iola said. "I don't want anyone to see me with a green-haired brother!" she said with a laugh.

Sunday morning after breakfast, Frank and Joe met Chet on Mike Mendez's block.

"My mom made me wash my hair over and over," Chet complained. His hair was a much lighter green than the day before.

The boys walked up to Mike's house. Frank rang the Mendezes' doorbell. Mrs. Mendez opened the door.

"Good morning, Mrs. Mendez," Frank said. "Is Mike home?"

Mrs. Mendez shook her head. "Mike has piano lessons on Sunday mornings."

"When will he be back?" Joe asked.

Mrs. Mendez looked at her watch. "In about ten minutes. Would you like to wait in his room until he returns?"

"You bet!" Frank cried. "I mean, that would be fine, Mrs. Mendez."

Mrs. Mendez pointed the way to Mike's room.

"I've never been in Mike's room before," Joe said as he opened the door.

The first thing they saw was a long table covered with glass beakers, clay robots, and many other odd-looking gadgets.

"This isn't a room," Chet gasped. "It's a mad scientist's lab!"

"I'm going to look on his shelves for the missing tape," Frank said.

"And I'm going to look for Frankenstein," Joe said, walking over to the table.

He studied the glass beakers on the table. Suddenly his eyes opened wide. One beaker was filled with a bright green substance.

"Hey, you guys," Joe called to Frank and Chet. "Check this out."

Frank ran over and looked in the beaker. "That looks like the same green stuff we found on the locker-room floor."

Joe reached in and touched it. "Feels like it, too."

Frank waved his hands. "Don't touch it, Joe! It might get—"

"Stuck!" Joe cried. "It's stuck to my hand!"

"Let me see," Chet said, grabbing Joe's hand.

"Chet—don't!" Frank pleaded.

"Oh, no. The green slime's got me. I'm stuck, too!" Chet moaned.

"Serves you right," Frank said. "I told you not to—"

Chet laughed and surprised Frank with a high-five. Now Frank had the sticky goo on his hands, too.

"What is this stuff, anyway?" Frank asked.

Suddenly the boys heard a loud cranking noise. Then a huge net fell from the ceiling. It covered them like a big brown spider's web!

"Ahhh!" Chet screamed.

"We're trapped!" Joe hollered.

"Gotcha." It was Mike, back from his piano lesson.

"What's the big idea?" Frank demanded, tugging at the net.

"I rigged that to protect my top-secret experiments," Mike explained.

"Great!" Joe groaned. "Now how about getting us out of here?"

Mike yanked a string, which pulled the net back up. "Why are you suddenly so interested in my inventions? You said they were weird."

Frank got right to the point. "We're looking for the thief who stole the tape of Friday's tryouts."

"I didn't know the tape was missing," Mike said.

Joe pulled the red plastic decoder ring from his jacket pocket. "Then how do you explain this?"

"My Crispy Creatures ring," Mike said. "I was wondering where I lost it."

"We found it inside one of the gloves of the Gulliver costume," Frank said.

"A mystery mascot was holding the camera before the tape disappeared," Joe said.

Chet held up his green, sticky palms. "We also found this gunk on the locker-room floor."

"Was that *you* inside the Gulliver costume?" Frank asked Mike.

Mike nodded slowly. "I did put the costume on. And I was in the costume when Joe handed me the camera. But I didn't steal any tape."

"Why did you put on my Gulliver costume?" Chet asked.

Mike took a deep breath. "I needed some kind of disguise. I wanted to get even with you guys for making fun of my spring sneakers."

"What were you planning to do?" Joe demanded.

"I was planning to coat your locker handles with Icky Sticky," Mike explained.

"Icky Sticky?" Frank repeated. "You mean this green stuff on our hands?"

Mike nodded. "I had a bottle of it in my knapsack on Friday afternoon. But when I dripped some on the locker-room floor, I got nervous and changed my mind."

"I get it," Frank said. "That's when

you took the costume off, dropped it on the floor—"

"—and ran out the exit door," Joe added.

Mike stared at Frank and Joe. "How did you guys know that?"

Joe shrugged. "We're the Clues Brothers, remember?"

"And I'm their detective-in-training," Chet said, taking a bow.

"I didn't steal the tape," Mike insisted. "And if you don't believe me, I invented a lie detector that I can use on myself."

"A lie detector?" Joe gasped. "You've invented *everything!*"

Mike nodded. "I even invented something to get that stuff off your hands."

"We don't blame you for being mad at us, Mike," Frank said.

"Yeah," Chet added. "I didn't mean to call your sneakers weird."

Mike picked up a metal hat with an electronic propeller. "I guess some of my inventions are kind of weird at that."

"Now we know who the mystery mascot was." Frank sighed. "But we still don't know who stole the tape."

Chet rubbed his growling stomach. "How about discussing this at Pizza Paradise? I always think better over mozzarella cheese."

Mrs. Mendez needed to get some groceries on Bay Street so she drove everyone to Pizza Paradise. While Mrs. Mendez went shopping, the boys sat at a table in the back of the pizza parlor.

"So, who do you think stole the tape?" Mike asked as the boys were munching on pieces of pepperoni pizza with extra cheese.

"I have no idea." Frank held up the detective book. "And I'm clean out of plans."

Joe flipped over his paper cup. "I'm clean out of soda. Let's get more drinks."

When Frank and Joe got to the counter they spotted Kevin Saris by the window. He was using his fist to pound on a huge wad of dough.

"Hi, Kevin," Joe called over the counter.

Kevin turned around. "Hi, Frank. Hi, Joe," he said quietly.

"What are you up to?" Frank asked.

"I'm learning how to make a pizza. Watch this." Kevin picked up the flattened dough and flipped it in the air.

"Neat!" Joe cried.

"What else do you do here while your parents are working?" Frank asked Kevin.

"Usually homework," Kevin said.

Mrs. Saris appeared behind the counter. "Kevin? Why don't you tell the boys about your video collection?"

Kevin stopped pouring tomato sauce on his dough. "It's no big deal, Ma."

Frank noticed that Kevin suddenly looked scared.

"Yes, it is, Kevin," Mrs. Saris said, wiping her hands on her apron. "You have the best video collection in Bayport."

Videos, Frank thought. Why is Kevin acting so strange over a video collection?

"Can we see your videos?" Frank asked.

Mrs. Saris stepped out from behind the counter. "Follow me, boys. In the back."

Kevin waved his hands. They were dripping with tomato sauce and shredded cheese. "Don't, Ma! Please."

Chet, Mike, Frank, and Joe followed Mrs. Saris into a room in the back of the store.

"Here is the VCR," Mrs. Saris said. She pointed to a shelf above the VCR. "And these are Kevin's videos."

The boys looked at the titles of the videos on the shelf.

"Wow! Kevin has three Jimmy Han action movies. And the latest Star Battle video!" Joe exclaimed.

Frank traced the videos with his finger. "Here's *Wild West Weekend, Captain Fearless*, and one called . . . " His voice trailed off.

"What is it, Frank?" Joe asked.

" . . . *Bayport Gulls Tryout Game!*"

8

Gulls Are Going to Fly

That's the missing tape!" Joe gasped.

"Don't be mad. I didn't mean to take it," Kevin said.

Everyone turned to see Kevin standing at the door.

"What is going on here?" Mrs. Saris asked.

Frank and Joe explained everything that happened in the gym on Friday.

"*You* took the tape, Kevin?" Mrs. Saris said, turning to Kevin.

"I found the video camera in the locker room after the game," Kevin explained. "There was no one around so I opened the camera and took out the tape."

"I don't get it," Joe said. "Chet said he saw you at the snack table eating a frosted doughnut."

Kevin shrugged. "I just took a few bites. Then I ate the rest on my way to the locker room."

Mrs. Saris looked upset. "Why on earth did you take the tape, Kevin?"

Kevin stared at the floor. "You were so angry when I was taken out of the game. Then I heard you say how you'd love to get your hands on Joe's tape."

Mrs. Saris looked embarrassed. "I didn't really mean that. I just wanted you to make the team, Kevin. You love basketball so much."

Kevin shook his head. "No, Mom.

You love basketball so much. Not me."

The room became very quiet.

"I had no idea that you felt that way," Mrs. Saris said. "Why didn't you tell me, Kevin?"

Kevin shrugged. "I tried to tell you. But I thought you wanted me to be a basketball star. I didn't want to let you down."

Mrs. Saris shook her head. "I can see now that I acted foolishly. You could never let me down, Kevin. You're a great kid."

She gave Kevin a big hug.

"Aw, Ma," Kevin said, blushing. "Not in front of the guys."

"From now on, I'm going to let you play whatever sport *you* want," Mrs. Saris declared.

Kevin smiled. "And from now on, I won't do anything stupid like steal anything."

He turned to Frank and Joe. "I'm sorry

I took the tape. I wish there was something I could do to make it up."

Joe thought for a second. Then his blue eyes lit up. "Come to think of it, that pizza you were making looked pretty good."

Kevin grinned. "All I have to do is pop it in the oven. Then there'll be more pizza for everyone."

"Did someone say, 'more pizza'?" Chet asked.

"We'll eat it here," Mike said.

"And we'll have one videotape to go," Joe said.

Frank and Joe gave each other a high five.

"Case closed!" Frank declared.

"This is Joe Hardy coming to you from the first Bayport Gulls game!" Joe said into the microphone of his video camera. "Coach Caruso is back, and the Gulls are ready to score."

It was two weeks later, and the Bayport Gulls were playing the Flying Catfish from the other elementary school in Bayport. Biff Hooper, a big boy with blond hair whom Frank and Joe had met when they first arrived at Bayport, was the center for the Catfish.

Frank, Tanya, and Zack had all made the Bayport Gulls. Joe's videotape had shown Coach Caruso that Dribbles *did* trip Frank. Dribbles made the team, but with a warning from the coach never to trip anyone again.

"Dribbles receives the ball," Joe said as the game began. "He passes it to Zack. Zack shoots and it's in. It's two more points for the Bayport Gulls!"

At the end of the second quarter, the Gulls were ahead by four points. The referee called time-out, and both teams trotted to their benches.

"While the Gulls take a breather, let's meet our fine-feathered mascot—Gulliver Morton!"

"*Arrrrk! Arrrrk!*" Chet shouted from

69

inside the Gulliver costume. "Bayport Gulls are gonna fly!"

Joe and Chet were joined by Frank. He wore his new blue-and-white Gulls uniform with a number 4 on the front and back.

"I'll bet over a hundred people are here today," Frank said.

Kevin Saris walked over, holding a pad and pencil. "Exactly two hundred and fifty-three people—and one baby," he corrected.

"What's up, Kevin?" Chet asked.

"I'm covering the game for the school newspaper," Kevin said proudly. "I always wanted to be a reporter."

"Kevin and I are a team," Joe said.

"Go, Kevin! Get the scoop!"

The boys looked up to see Mrs. Saris cheering from the bleachers. She sat next to Mr. and Mrs. Hardy and wore a new sweatshirt, which read, Kevin Saris, #1 Reporter!

Kevin grinned. "My mom's going to

hang all of my articles over the pizza counter."

Suddenly Dribbles Libretti pushed his way between Frank and Joe.

"Everyone is here to watch *me* play, twerps!" Dribbles shouted.

"Hey, Dribbles!" came a voice.

The boys turned to see Mike Mendez. He was holding a basketball in front of him with the tips of his fingers.

"Catch!" Mike shouted.

Dribbles received the ball. He reached out to dribble, but the ball didn't move. It was stuck to his hand.

"What's the big idea?" Dribbles cried.

Mike chuckled. "It's just what you'd call a *sticky* situation!"

"An Icky Sticky situation," Joe added.

Tanya, Biff, Zack, and other players from both teams surrounded Dribbles and laughed.

"Will somebody get this thing off of me?" Dribbles shouted frantically.

Chet shook his tail and squawked. *"Arrrrk! Arrrrk! Arrrrk!"*

"Wow," Kevin said. "This is going to be a great story."

Joe pointed his camera at Dribbles and pushed the green button.

". . . and a totally *awesome* video!"

TAKE A RIDE
WITH THE KIDS ON BUS FIVE!

Natalie Adams and James Penny have just started
third grade. They like their teacher, and they like
Maple Street School. The only trouble is, they have
to ride bad old Bus Five to get there!

#1 THE BAD NEWS BULLY
Can Natalie and James stop the bully on Bus Five?

#2 WILD MAN AT THE WHEEL
When Mr. Balter calls in sick,
the kids get some strange new drivers.

#3 FINDERS KEEPERS
The kids on Bus Five keep losing things.
Is there a thief on board?

#4 I SURVIVED ON BUS FIVE
Bad luck turns into big fun
when Bus Five breaks down in a rainstorm.

BY MARCIA LEONARD
ILLUSTRATED BY JULIE DURRELL

A MINSTREL® BOOK
Published by Pocket Books

1237-04

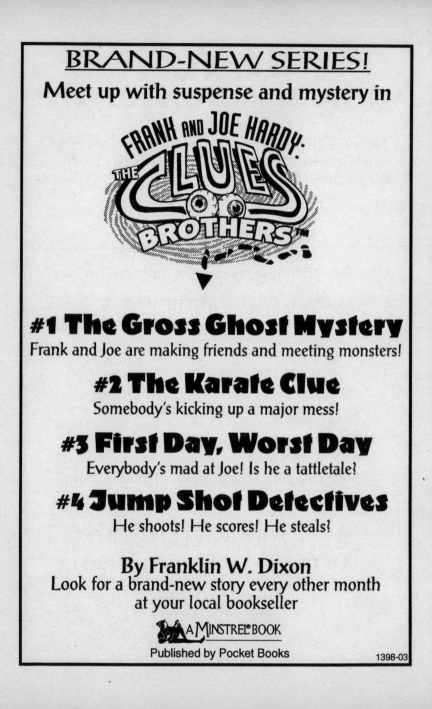

BRAND-NEW SERIES!

Meet up with suspense and mystery in

FRANK AND JOE HARDY:
THE CLUES BROTHERS™

#1 The Gross Ghost Mystery

Frank and Joe are making friends and meeting monsters!

#2 The Karate Clue

Somebody's kicking up a major mess!

#3 First Day, Worst Day

Everybody's mad at Joe! Is he a tattletale?

#4 Jump Shot Detectives

He shoots! He scores! He steals!

By Franklin W. Dixon

Look for a brand-new story every other month
at your local bookseller

A MINSTREL® BOOK

Published by Pocket Books

1398-03